Jingle His Bells

Kaci Rose

Copyright

Copyright © 2022, by Kaci Rose, Five Little Roses Publishing. All Rights Reserved.

No part of this publication may be reproduced, distributed,

or transmitted in any form or by any means, including photocopying, recording,

or other electronic or mechanical methods, or by any information storage and

retrieval system without the prior written permission of the publisher, except

in the case of very brief quotations embodied in critical reviews and certain

other noncommercial uses permitted by copyright law.

Publisher's Note: This is a work of fiction. Names,

characters, places, and incidents are a product of the author's imagination.

Locales and public names are sometimes

used for atmospheric purposes. Any resemblance to actual people, living or dead, or to businesses, companies, events, institutions, or locales is completely coincidental.

Book Cover By: **Cormar Covers**
Editing By: Debbe @ **On The Page, Author and PA Services**

Contents

Get Free Books!	VII
1. Chapter 1	1
2. Chapter 2	9
3. Chapter 3	18
4. Chapter 4	28
5. Chapter 5	35
6. Chapter 6	40
7. Chapter 7	44
8. Chapter 8	48
9. Chapter 9	53
10. Chapter 10	58
11. Epilogue	61
12. Other Books by Kaci Rose	65
13. Connect with Kaci Rose	68
14. About Kaci Rose	70

Please Leave a Review!

Get Free Books!

Do you like Military Men? Best friends brothers?
What about sweet, sexy, and addicting books?

If you join Kaci Rose's Newsletter you get these books free!

https://www.kacirose.com/free-books/
Now on to the story!

Chapter 1

Emma

"That spineless, useless bastard!" I screech.

My best friend Kayla doesn't even ask, she simply plucks my phone from my hands to read the text my boyfriend just sent me.

Sorry, ex-boyfriend.

Brody: Don't want to do this anymore. We need to break up.

"What the hell?" She says once she's read it too.

Brody and I have been dating since our junior year of high school. We then went off to the same college together and we're both seniors there. We came home this week to have Christmas with our families. He got in two days ago because he finished all his exams, but I had one last exam to take so I got in earlier today.

Kayla has always lived next door to me, so the moment my car pulled in, she was in my room helping me get settled and catching up. That's when this lovely text came in.

"It's been almost six years, and he's going to end it in a text? He really is spineless." She tosses my phone on my bed and looks at me.

I know she's waiting for me to process my feelings about what just happened, and I'm trying.

"I'm more pissed off that he broke up with me via text than the fact that he actually broke up with me. What does that tell you about where our relationship has been?" I flop down on the bed next to her.

"I know you have been on the fence for a while and maybe he has too. You deserved an in person discussion, but what's done is done." She picks up my phone and her thumbs fly across the screen. A minute later she hands me the phone and I see she has responded to Brody.

Me: Glad we are on the same page, only I was going to do it in person. Best of luck.

"What was the point of that?" I ask her.

"So that he knows that you got it and to confirm the breakup. Because I'm not going to let you sit here and wallow over Christmas break," she says.

Knowing Kayla, I'm sure that means she already has a plan. One that she won't let me back out of whether I want to or not.

"And what does that plan include?"

"First, you're going to get dressed up in something cute and sexy. We are going to Club Red."

"What?" I ask in shock.

"Listen, we both know Brody wasn't fulfilling you in bed. That's why the books you read keep getting dirtier and dirtier. You forget we share an eBook library. I see what you read, and full disclosure, I read most of it myself. So, let's go and explore our kinky side as a fuck you to the whole situation."

She isn't wrong about the books, or Brody. Things used to be good between us, I think. Just lately he's been distant, as have I. When we have sex, it's the same two positions every time. Even worse, he hasn't cared if I get off, only that he does.

"Damn, I should have left his ass a long time ago." I sigh and Kayla nods her head.

She walks across my room to my closet. I may be in college but my room here at my parents' hasn't changed. Everything I don't take with me to school, I still have here.

As Kayla goes through my closet, she finds a black leather skintight dress that I wore as part of a Halloween costume one year and pulls it out.

"I'm not wearing that." I shake my head.

"Yes, you are, and you will still be overdressed," she says.

"You've been before?"

"I saw a guy last year, and we went a few times. He had a membership and I still have member privileges, so get moving. We have a bit of a drive into the city."

We grew up in a small suburb of Chicago, but Club Red is downtown, so it will take us some time to get there. My parents are out at some dinner tonight with friends so they won't be home until late, so why not go and check it out?

I have to admit, I'm curious to see if it's anything like the books I've read about BDSM clubs. Taking the dress Kayla is holding up, I sigh as I reach for it.

"I'll go get dressed and be back to do your hair." She jumps up and runs next door to her parents' place as I reluctantly slide on the dress.

It's tight and hugs every curve of my body. What can I say? I'm a curvy girl and I can't remember the last time I had any kind of a thigh gap. But even in this slinky dress, I think I look pretty damn good.

When Kayla walks back into the room, I'm sitting down and applying my makeup.

"Damn girl! I don't swing that way, but if I did, I'd do you!"

This isn't the first time she's said that and I get it's a compliment, even if I know it's not exactly true.

"Good thing I don't swing that way either, or I might take you up on it." I joke back to her, but my nerves shine through.

She wastes no time curling my hair. Kayla is a genius with hair, so I've always given her free rein styling my hair. For me, putting effort is tossing it up in a ponytail.

Before I know it, we are in downtown Chicago and standing outside what looks like a warehouse with the word 'Red' above the doors in neon letters. You can't even see a hint of light shining though, because the glass door has a dark tint. So, when Kayla opens the door, I wasn't expecting the bright white reception room we are entering.

There is a woman in jeans and a t-shirt at a desk and two men standing before a set of double doors at the far end of the room.

The lady at the desk hands me a stack of papers to read and sign. While I'm completing the paperwork, she and Kayla chat.

The paperwork consists of stacks of consent forms. Stuff like you must adhere to the rules, making sure you understand stop doesn't mean stop, that there is video surveillance in the non-private rooms, and finally, there is security everywhere.

There are papers on how to get help if needed, but also the consequences of breaking up a scene or doing something without a person's consent.

There is yet another page on safe words and how red means to stop, yellow means getting close to hitting a limit and green means good to go. Then I get to the paper with the monthly and yearly dues and my stomach drops at the prices. Thankfully, I'm only here as a guest for the next week while I'm home for Christmas break because there is no way I couldn't afford these prices still being in school. Once I hand over the papers, Kayla takes my hand and leads me toward the two men by the double doors who look like massive NFL football players.

They open the door for us and that's when the music fills room and we step from the bright white office to the darker main room. The room has black concrete floors, black walls, and black furniture. There are red accents everywhere.

To the right is the large bar and in front of us is the largest black leather sectional I've ever seen. It easily seats thirty people with room to spare. At the far end of the room is a stage, but it's currently dark. Looking up, the ceiling is over three stories high, with glass windows that look like the side of an office building going up the length of the wall and looking down at the main room.

"Those are the themed play rooms on the second floor and on the third floor are the private rooms. Come on, let's get you a drink. You are going to need it." Kayla says, dragging me to the bar.

She orders us a drink and the bartenders gives me the once over before handing me my drink and moving on to the next person. When I turn around to look at the room, a scene on the couch catches my attention.

A man with a woman kneeling between his legs is giving him a blow job. Sitting right next to them is a woman with her man on his knees, eating her out for the whole world to see. What caught my eye is the man and woman on the couch who are making out while their partners are giving them oral. This place is wild.

But I'm pulled from the scene when a man steps up beside me. I turn to tell him I'm not interested, only I see the last person I ever expected standing there.

Zion.

My ex-boyfriend Brody's older brother.

Chapter 2

Zion

What the hell is Emma doing here?

Has she lost her damn mind?

Sweet, innocent Emma here at Club Red?

She will be eaten alive. Several other doms took notice of her the second she walked into the room. With her eyes full of wonder, she broadcasts how new she is here. If Kayla hadn't been there, they would have been all over her.

I can't let that happen. Not just because she's my brother's girlfriend. He may be family, but that asshole brought a new girl home for Christmas. When we got into a fight about how he should have broken up with Emma first, I escaped here to Club Red. My safe haven.

I don't know what my brother was thinking, to have a girl as sweet and caring as Emma and to cheat on her. It made me so angry, I lost it. Even though I have always had feelings for Emma, she was my brother's girl and I couldn't do a damn thing about it. But at least it meant she'd be around for the holidays, and I could spend time with her. All I wanted was for her to be happy, even if it's with my brother.

Brody swore he'd break up with her tomorrow when they get together and I have to take him at his word. But seeing her here now, I don't know if I can not tell her what is going on. Emma always has this way of pulling the truth from me.

"What are you doing here, Emma?"

"Well, your asshole brother broke up with her via text earlier today. So I dragged her butt out here because there is no way in hell he's ruining her Christmas," Kayla answered.

But I can't take my eyes off Emma. Her blond hair is curled and flowing over her shoulders. The black dress she's wearing pushes her breasts up and hugs every curve. It's so tight it looks like it was painted on her. I'm thankful she is wearing more clothes than the other women around here. I don't like the idea of other guys seeing her like this.

But when I hear my brother broke up with her, mixed emotions fill me.

First, I'm pissed that he dumped her via text. She deserves so much more than that. Then I'm ecstatic that he's no longer with her and she's now single. I knew Emma wouldn't be the kind to cheat, so her being here while still with my brother didn't make sense. I'm curious as to why she's here, but excited that she might be interested. Though I'm determined that I'm the one that will be showing her around.

"You ever been here before?" I ask her, trying to keep my voice light but neutral.

She shakes her head nervously and takes a sip of her drink. Good, I didn't think she was interested in anything Club Red had to offer, but if she was, there won't be anyone else but me showing her around. I couldn't stand it.

"Come on, princess. Let me show you around then." I hold my hand up. It's up to her if she takes it. I'm sure she was given a list of rules just like I was, but I'm going to make sure.

She hesitates for just a moment, and my heart races faster than I can ever remember, hoping that she will take my hand. When she reaches out and her hand lands in mine, I feel like she just gave me the entire world.

"I'll watch out for her," I tell Kayla, who nods at me and shoots me a wink before turning back to the bar. Kayla is an observant one and I get a feeling she might know my feelings for Emma, even if she'll never confront me about them.

With Emma's hand in mine, it's a signal to the other doms to leave her alone. I know there's no way I'm taking her upstairs to the more intense rooms. Right now, I want to see how she reacts out here in the main area. Plus, I don't want her to feel uncomfortable by taking her to a more enclosed area.

"So, what out here catches your attention?" I ask and watch for even the slightest sign from her.

"Well, everything. There are people having sex right next to you over there on the couch." Even with the dimmer lights, I can still tell her face is turning a beautiful shade of pink.

I chuckle and shake my head.

"There has to be some reason that you decided to come tonight. What turns you on, baby girl?"

She zeroes in on the Saint Andrews cross. A woman is tied to it as her partner makes her cum over and over again. As she watches, her breathing picks up and even through the tight dress, I can tell her nipples get hard.

"What about that couple turns you on? Her being strapped down? Or him making her cum in front of everyone?" I ask.

Her wide eyes turn to me. "I'm not sure," she whispers barely loud enough for me to hear.

"Care to find out?" I tease. Even though I shouldn't, as I've been fighting a massive hard on ever since I saw her in that dress sitting there at the bar like the perfect little girl I always imagined her to be.

So, when she nods, I swear I could almost cum in my pants from the thought alone. She doesn't know how much she affects me, so I take a deep breath to regain my composure and step into my dominant side.

Scanning the room, I find a spot along the wall. It will give us a bit of privacy, but still the thrill that she wants. So I lead her over there and she seems to take comfort putting her back to the wall.

"Can I touch you?" I ask wanting to make consent very clear. She nods her head, but that's not enough.

"I need your words, baby girl."

"Yes, you can touch me." She says with more confidence than I expected.

Taking both of her hands in mine, I raise them above her head. Then I trap her wrists in one of my hands against the wall. I slowly trail the other hand down her arm, over her shoulder and her breasts until she tenses up. I pause and get her eyes on me.

"Do you remember what your safe words are?" I ask.

She nods.

"What are they?" I need to make sure.

"Green if I'm good, yellow when I'm close to a limit and red to stop." She whispers so I'm the only one to hear it.

"Do you want to use a safe word?" I ask.

She just shakes her head.

"Okay then, relax for me."

She takes a deep breath, and as she lets it out, her body relaxes. Slowly, I move my hand down her body, over her stomach to the edge of her dress. Pausing for a moment to let my intent sink in, I give her a chance to stop me, but she doesn't.

With languid movements, I pull her dress up and reach under it, coming in contact with her wet panties.

"You do like what you were seeing, huh, baby girl?" I say, watching for every little reaction. If hadn't been looking at her so closely, I wouldn't have noticed the slight nod she gives me.

I stoke her over the panties which are separating us, before pulling them to the side and running a finger over her clit. Her eyes flutter closed, and her head falls back against the wall. There is a crushing need in me to have her eyes, so I know she isn't thinking of anyone else.

"Eyes open." I snap harsher than I mean to. Her eyes pop open and they lock on me.

I continue to play with her clit as she squirms. The entire atmosphere must have had her more turned on than she realized because a moment later she starts to cum. Not wanting to draw too much attention to her, I lean in and kiss her, swallowing any noises she makes.

"Fuck, that was hot," I tell her when she relaxes. Then I pull her into my arms, carrying her to the couch where I set her in my lap, allowing me to offer some aftercare.

Even though I know I shouldn't touch her, I can't help it. I'm so damn addicted to her now.

"Looks like you had some fun. You ready to head home?" Kayla bounces over way sooner than I'd like.

Emma simply looks up at me before letting her friend lead her from the club.

Fuck, I thought I was in deep before.

• • • • ● • ● • • •

The next day I don't think I've gotten any sleep. Instead, I relive that moment with her over and over again, trying to get some relief to my cock, who seems to be permanently hard now.

At the club tonight, I'm supposed to give a demonstration with a sub. But touching another woman now seems wrong and I know I can't do it.

So, I call my buddy, Hunter, who helped get me into the lifestyle. I explain who Emma is and what happened last night and how I'm feeling about her. He listens patiently to it all.

"Well, don't force yourself to do anything tonight. I'll take over your demonstration. As far as the girl is concerned, you know how I feel. As long as it's consensual, fuck everyone else."

"But it's wrong," I protest.

"Says who?" he asks.

"She dated my brother."

"That's a reason. Still doesn't answer my question."

JINGLE HIS BELLS

I try to think. I've told a few people over the years about Emma and nobody has said it's wrong.

"You silence says everything."

"Should I call her or not?" I sigh, wanting direction.

"What the hell is this? High school?"

"I think I've been in love with her since then."

He pauses for a moment. "Call her, but have a game plan."

Chapter 3

Emma

I'm out Christmas shopping with Kayla since I had zero time to do so before coming home. Between classes and finals, Christmas shopping was the last thing on my mind. Now I'm wishing I had thought more about it because I have no idea what to get everyone.

So here we are walking around the mall two towns over because it's bigger and has a better selection of stores. In between shopping, Kayla asked a ton of questions about last night and I was more than happy to talk because I am so far out of my element, it's not even funny.

"I feel like I should text, but I have no idea what. Hey thanks for making me cum in front of a room full of people. Hope you are having a great day?" I say, making Kayla laugh.

"Well, yes to texting him. If you want to and like what happened, then do it. But maybe something like, hey I had a great time last night. Thanks for showing me around."

I pull out my phone and give it a shot.

Me: Thank you for showing me around last night. I had a great time.

We barely get into the next shop before my phone goes off.
"Wow, I don't know what I was expecting, but it wasn't that." I say, showing Kayla my phone.

Zion: I'm glad you enjoyed yourself, baby girl. Because I did too. If you want to come back again, I'm happy to show you around.

"Well, do you want to go back?" Kayla asks.
"Yeah, I think I do."
"Then do it. You have two free weeks without school, stress, and worries. Enjoy yourself."
I know she's right.

Me: I'd like to go back. If you really mean it.
Zion: Of course, I do. There is a presentation on the stage tonight if you are available. I think you'll really like it.

"He wants to meet tonight. Says there is some presentation I'd like?" I tell Kayla, who squeals and causes everyone around us to turn and look to see what is going on.

"You should go for sure." She says with a huge smile.

"But I don't have anything to wear." I wail, knowing exactly what's going to come out of her mouth next.

"Guess it's a good thing we're at a mall full of clothes. Let's find you something."

"What about Christmas shopping?"

"Since I know your mom and your dad pretty well, I'll pick up a few things. But you still have a few more days before Christmas. Let me take what you've already gotten and I'll wrap it up. Come on, you deserve this."

Me: Well, how can a girl say no to an excuse to buy a new outfit?

Zion: Get something red and wear a short skirt, no panties.

"I do love a man who knows what he wants," Kayla says as she drags me to a store that seems to have more of the clothes that you would see people wearing at Club Red.

JINGLE HIS BELLS 21

The rest of the afternoon is a whirlwind as I buy my outfits and head home, sending up a silent prayer that my parents happen to be having dinner at a friend's tonight. So I don't have to try to hide what I'm wearing when I leave the house. If my parents are up when I get home, I grab something I can put over my clothes.

Later that night when I step in to Club Red, I feel eyes on me and not in a creepy way. But more of a comforting way. It only takes a few minutes before I find out those eyes belong to Zion and our eyes lock as he makes his way across the room to me.

"Can I touch you, baby girl?" He asks as he steps in front of me.

"Yes," I tell him and nod my head, which gets me a smile.

He takes my hand and leads me to the back of the room towards the stage where the Saint Andrews cross is set up. A small crowd has gathered, but the presentation has yet to start.

"You're early and I like that. Good girl for listening to my instructions. But did you listen to all of them?"

"Maybe you should find out," I say and immediately bite my lip.

This sexy, flirty girl is not me. I'm normally shy and more reserved. But something about last night with him was freeing. I feel more relaxed around him.

He pulls me over to a slightly oversized leather chair. Then he seats me right on his lap as the show starts. A woman in a short silk robe walks out on stage, followed by a man who is shirtless and wearing nothing but a pair of black sweatpants.

As the man removes the woman's robe and ties her to the Saint Andrews cross, Zion's hand travel up the inside of my thigh. He pushes the tight black miniskirt up as his hand snakes beneath it to find out I have indeed followed his orders and not worn any underwear.

I looked over at him to find him watching me.

"Eyes on the stage." He says in a commanding voice that I can't help but obey.

As I watch the show on the stage, it barely registers what's going on. All I can feel is Zion and his hands on me. He's playing with me so slowly that it's teasing me, making me want more.

In the blink of an eye, it seems the show is over and I couldn't tell you a single thing that happened on the stage.

"Let's head upstairs. I rented us a room." He whispers in my ear, and I nod.

He leads me upstairs past a much smaller sitting area and down a candlelit hall to a room where he punches in a code. When I walk in, I'm immediately hit with large floor to ceiling windows that overlook the area downstairs we were just in.

"I can close the curtains if it's too overwhelming." He says as I walk over and step in front of them.

"I think I'd like that," I tell him.

Nodding, he walks to a panel on the wall, pushes a button and the windows go black. I finally get a chance to look around the room. There's a bed in the center against one wall, a couch and the Saint Andrews cross against the other wall and cabinets full of toys and playthings.

"You remember your safe words?" he asks again.

I nod. "Just like a traffic light. Pretty easy to remember."

He smirks while unbuttoning his shirt and his eyes are on me.

"I really like this outfit on you. It's not anything I would have ever expected to see you wearing, but in a way it's still very much you. But I just think it'll look much better on the floor." He steps to me, placing his hands on my hips and slowly drags the skirt zipper down.

He removes my clothes with ease and his lips land on mine as he backs me up against the St. Andrews Cross. Then, taking my hands in his, he stretches them out on the cross, stopping to look at me.

"You are doing okay, baby girl?" His eyes search my face.

"Yes, I'm still green," I tell him, and he smirks.

He reaches over and straps both of my hands to the cross. Getting on his knees in front of me, he takes my legs and spreads each of them before strapping them to the cross.

Then he runs his hands up the inside of my thighs, where everything is on full display. If I had the ability, I know I'd be closing my legs right now.

He smirks, almost as if he knows what I'm thinking. "I like having you exposed just for me. You're so fucking beautiful."

Leaning into me, his tongue makes contact with my clit, and I cry out because after all the teasing downstairs, it feels so damn good. I thought men that were this good with their tongue were an urban myth or something from romance novels. I've never been happier to be wrong. In minutes, he has me ready to cum, but instead he stops. I want to urge him to finish up when he removes his clothes and walks to the nightstand to get a condom.

"This is the last time I'm going to check in with you, baby girl. I expect you to use your safe words if you need them," he orders.

"Still green," I whisper as I run my eyes over his sculpted abs that look just as good as they did by the pool last summer.

He nods and puts the condom on and walks over to me.

"Press your back to the cross, baby girl. Relax."

I do as he asks, and that's when I realize he hasn't tied my arms down as tight as I thought. There is some give, but not enough to reach out and touch him. As he steps between my legs, I also find out the top part of the cross reclines just enough that it spreads me open for him.

Now, I'm at the perfect angle for his cock to rest at my opening. Our eyes lock and for a moment, and we're both thinking we shouldn't be doing this. But then, without a word being spoken, he thrusts inside of me. He isn't gentle, but he isn't too rough either.

Without a doubt, this isn't lovemaking. This is sex, fucking hot, raw sex. Nothing emotional. Though I can't tell you the last time sex felt this damn good. Being tied up somehow heightens all the feelings because I'm not concentrating on where to put my hands or my legs, I'm focused solely on what he is doing to me.

Every thrust, every drag in and out of me, I feel his thick cock. His hands trailing up my breasts and his thumbs running over my nipples feel like exquisite torture. As he places kisses on my neck, I feel his strong fingers gripping my hair and forcefully tilting my head up to look at him.

"Come for me now, Emma," he whispers, and it's as if my body was waiting for his permission.

I tense and the strongest orgasm I've ever felt in my life hits me like a tsunami. I'm barely aware of him cumming right along with me. My body trembles at the intense sensation running through me.

One moment I'm feeling the most amazing pleasure, and the next I'm sitting on Zion's lap on the couch wrapped in a blanket, not sure how I got there.

"There she is." He smiles and his soft side is back as he rubs me gently while pulling me close with the other.

"What happened?" I ask, snuggling into him.

"I think you hit subspace for a moment. You were so relaxed and in your own little world." He kisses the top of my head.

"I should probably get going... " I start to say, not sure what to do next.

"No, now you're going to sit here and let me take care of you. Aftercare is a big part of all this, especially for someone new to it like you. Even more so in our situation."

I think I'm really going to like aftercare.

Chapter 4

Zion

I'm not sure how my parents convinced me to have dinner with my brother and his new girl, but I think they are just trying to keep the peace after the bombshell he dropped about bringing this girl home.

I'm sitting at the table and all I can think about is how Brody downgraded when he took this girl over Emma. Where Emma is sweet, caring, and thoughtful, she's crass and rude. They look like one of those couples you know is only together for sex.

That thought takes me back to last night with Emma. I shouldn't have touched her, but fuck, I can't regret it. Last night was the single most amazing moment in my life and I was up until all hours trying to figure out how to make it happen again.

JINGLE HIS BELLS

The new girl's giggle fills the air, and it's like nails on a chalkboard. Staring at the two of them, I'm disgusted. I can't even remember her name. All I can think about is how Emma should be here and how much I loved family dinners when she was here, even if she was with him instead of me.

This new girl keeps talking down to my parents even when she is wrong about the subject they are discussing. Then there is the fact that Brody can't stop staring at her boobs. His fascination with her tits could partly be because this girl is dressed extremely inappropriately for a family dinner. Hell, prostitutes that stand on the corner and try to flag you down wear more clothes than she is.

When I volunteer to do the dishes to avoid both of them, my mom gives me a look saying she knows exactly what I'm doing, but she will allow it so she can get out of washing them.

Unfortunately, Brody's new girl seems very excited to clear off the table and be helpful. It doesn't take long to find out why.

"I just love a man who does dishes." She slithers over to me, setting down the plate she just brought in.

"Then you are out of luck with my brother. I doubt he's cleaned a dish in his entire life." I tell her, moving away to the other side of the kitchen to put the leftovers from dinner away.

"Well, I prefer an older man, anyway." She slides up beside me again, this time pressing her very fake boobs against my arm.

I took a huge step back and away from her.

"Listen here... Cindy," I say, trying to remember her name.

"Candy." She corrects me, not that it's much better.

"You are here with my brother. Leave me the fuck alone." I tell her bluntly, and she has the audacity to look like I slapped her across the face.

Of course, that's the moment my mother walks in as well.

"Zion, I know I raised you better than that."

"You raised Brody better than to cheat on his girlfriend and bring this girl home before he broke up with the last one. But no one's talking about that."

Candy's eyes go wide. Even though she doesn't say a word, I'm guessing that was news to her.

JINGLE HIS BELLS 31

"I'm going for a walk." I don't even wait for an answer as I head out the back door and take the trail that leads toward the small creek my dad and I would go fishing in during the summer.

When I reach the creek, I stay there for a minute, taking a few deep breaths and decide it's probably best I go to my home. I can come back and apologize to my mom and dad some other time. But with Brody staying here with Candy, it's probably not a good thing for me to be there much longer.

When I get back to the house, Dad is standing at the edge of the yard at the trail waiting for me.

"I figured if you were heading to the creek you needed to get your thoughts together." He says as I join him.

"Yeah, I don't know how you guys seem okay with all of this. Emma was part of the family and the way he treated her, well, I just can't forgive him for it so easily."

"What do you mean?" Dad asks.

"I ran into Emma the other night. When Brody got here with Candy, he was still dating Emma. When I confronted him about it, he broke up with her via text. Apparently, he's been cheating on Emma for a while. She doesn't know that, and I didn't have the heart to tell her."

"Why does it bother you so much what Brody did to Emma?" Dad asks as he watches and waits for my response. He's like me. He knows a person says just as much with their body language as they do with their words.

Dad and I have been very close and I've always shared things with him that I might not have shared with other people, so I decided to be honest and open with him. Maybe he'll have some advice for me.

"I've always liked Emma. More than just oh, she's the girl that my brother is dating. I was going to ask her out before Brody did, but he got wind of it and asked her out as a joke, and she said yes. But I never expected them to date this long. The more time she spent here, the more my feelings for her grew. And now..."

I stopped myself. Dad and I have a very open relationship, and he knows about Club Red. Even though he doesn't always understand, he supports me the best way he can, by being my sounding board when I need it.

"And now that she and Brody aren't together you want to make a move?" He tries to fill in the last of my thoughts.

"I already have. She showed up at Club Red the other night. Her friend Kayla brought her, and I showed her around. She came back last night, and we had a scene together."

"As in you had sex?" he asks.

"Yes. Then after she let me hold her, and we talked for hours before I helped her home. My feelings for her were strong before, but now? Fuck, I crossed that line, and I can't go back."

"Do you want to know what I think?" he asks.

"Always."

"I think this is really Emma's choice. She's an adult and so are you. I want both of you to be happy and if that means being happy together, so be it. Emma has always fit in with this family. But so help me God, do not ever repeat to Brody that he never deserved her."

My entire body relaxes, and I sigh. To know at least my dad is on my side makes things a lot easier.

"So, are you out here hiding from Candy as well?" He asks obviously trying to lighten the topic.

"Damn right I am. That girl looks like she came right from the strip club to dinner."

We both burst out laughing and that's when Mom steps out on the porch. She smiles and waves at us, letting us know that our absence is starting to be noticed.

"You should go in, but put your best face forward to try to support your brother."

After going in, we hung out a bit longer before I went home.

Once in the car, I decided to text Emma and ask her out on a proper date. My brother be damned. I want her and I'm going after her.

Chapter 5

Emma

With the busy past few nights, it felt so good to sleep in. Especially since I fell asleep early watching a movie with Kayla. I didn't expect to wake up to a text from Zion that he sent last night.

Zion: Hope you aren't busy tomorrow. I'd like to take you out on a date.
Me: I hadn't planned to go to the club tonight because I'm having dinner with my parents.

Almost immediately, when I start getting ready for the day, my phone goes off.

Zion: Not at the club. I want to take you out for the day. It's a surprise. Will you go with me? I promise to take you home in time for dinner with your parents.

I stop and reread my phone several times before I respond. A day with Zion? I don't want to be too excited, but I defiantly don't want to pass that up either.

Me: That sounds like fun. Where should I meet you?
Zion: This is a date, baby girl. I'm picking you up. Is an hour enough time for you to get ready?
Me: Yes, but what do I wear?
Zion: Jeans and good walking shoes. See you soon.

I rush through getting ready and despite the cold weather, I am sitting on the porch with a cup of coffee when he pulls up.

"You should have waited inside where it's warm." He says, walking to me and reaching for my hand.

"I don't get a lot of fresh air at school, so I try to enjoy it when I'm home as much as possible."

He leads me to his car, where he opens the car door for me and waits for me to get settled before closing the door and getting into his side of the vehicle.

JINGLE HIS BELLS

"So, where are we going?" I'm excited to find out.

"You'll see. We have a little bit of a drive, but I know you'll love it."

While driving towards the city, we talk easily and catch up. When I'd be at his parents' house for dinners or hanging out in the summer, we spent a lot of time talking. Regardless of what happened at Club Red, it's nice to know that hasn't changed.

Though what does shock me is when we pull into the Christkindl Market. My jaw drops as I look over at him.

"I happen to know you visit every Christmas and collect their yearly mugs. So, I figured I'd like to be the one to take you this year." He shrugs like it's no big deal.

It's a huge deal. My parents started bringing me before I was old enough to walk and I've been collecting their yearly mugs ever since. I haven't missed a single year, but Brody didn't do shopping and hated coming down here. So, I'd either continue the tradition with my parents or with Kayla. The difference between the two brothers is night and day. It's becoming very clear I spent way too much time with the wrong brother.

"You've been paying attention." I get out of the car and take a moment to compose myself.

He's paid attention to the little things like I collect the mugs. Brody never remembered and always asked what was the point of coming down here every year.

"Well, I've always wanted to bring you, but it seemed inappropriate until now."

He takes my hand and lets me walk by every booth and vendor and patiently waits as I talk to them or as I simply browse all the items for sale.

We grab hot chocolate and lunch from the food trucks nearby and make a whole day out of it. He doesn't rush me, and we have a good fun time. He makes sure we get my mug and even points out a gift my mom would love.

All the time, he's holding my hand and finding little ways to touch me. He's still protective, watching me and guiding me through the crowd. I'm actually able to enjoy myself, instead of constantly having to be on alert.

"Thank you for this." I tell him on our way home.

"I had a great time and hope you did, too." He says, holding my hand as he drives.

"I had the best time. I don't think I've had so much fun at the Christkindl Market in a long time."

"Good. That's what I like to hear." He says with a big smile lighting up his face.

Both my parents are sitting on the front porch when we pull into the driveway. I haven't seen much of them. Heck, they don't even know Brody and I broke up.

I guess it's time to face the music.

Chapter 6

Emma

I was shocked my parents didn't start hounding me with questions the moment Zion pulled away. But they just said dinner would be ready in twenty minutes and let me go to my room with the bags of things I bought at the market.

"Dinner's ready!" Mom calls up the stairs.

I take one deep breath and head downstairs, knowing I won't get out of dinner so easily.

My mom made my favorite meal of meatloaf, mashed potatoes, bacon green beans, and rolls. Once everyone has food on their plates, they start in.

"How were finals?" Dad asks.

"Hard, but I think I did okay. We will know soon."

"You've been spending a lot of time with Brody since you have been back," Mom says.

JINGLE HIS BELLS 41

I have been out every night since I got home, and of course, they assume it's with Brody because I haven't been able to tell them otherwise.

"Actually Brody broke up with me the night I got home via text. Kayla took me out that night and I've spent the last few days with Zion."

They are quiet for a moment, before my mom asks, "Brody's older brother Zion?"

"Yes. I ran into him the other night and we've just clicked."

"What happened with Brody?" Dad asks.

"I'm not sure. It hasn't been right for a while. We started spending less and less time together. When he came home a few days before me, he didn't wait like usual for my last final. Then the day I got into town, I texted him to let him know and he texted back to break up with me. But I had been talking to Kayla about it, how it had felt off. After thinking about it, I'm not really heartbroken over it at all."

Things are quiet for a minute before Mom starts asking questions again.

"So, Zion?" she asks.

"We just connected the other night, and he took me to the Christkindl Market today. He let me stop at every booth and we had a great time." I tell them honestly.

"I've always liked Zion better than Brody. Zion has his head on straight. He's got a good mind for business and according to his father, he's got a few startup companies that are doing extremely well," Dad says.

"But wouldn't it be wrong to date Zion after I dated his brother?" I ask the question I've been waiting for them to ask.

"Oh, baby, only you can decide that. Zion has more to lose being it's his brother. So, this has to be his choice, too. If you choose each other, then it's no one's business but your own. But you need to talk to him about it," Mom says.

After dinner we get out the Christmas stuff and decorate the tree. It's been a family tradition for the three of us to do it together and Kayla always joins in, so it's no surprise when she comes over to help.

She's always been part of the family, and she's like the sister I never had. With her around, I never felt like an only child and I was never lonely with her right next door. Once the tree is decorated, Kayla and I go up to my room and I fill her in on what happened today and what my parents said at dinner.

"Well, I agree with your parents. Zion is definitely an upgrade. But it has to be both your choices, so you should talk to Zion. Who knows, maybe he only wants a holiday fling. Talk, so at least you are on the same page."

I know she's right. The problem is, I don't think I could take it if he only wanted a holiday fling. I've always had a crush on Zion, but I didn't think he had any interest in me. I was a few grades behind him in high school and then he went off to college. So seeing him at family events with Brody was all I got, and it had to be enough.

After being with him this past weekend at Club Red, I don't think it would be enough anymore.

Chapter 7

Zion

Tonight is the Christmas event at the Club, and I want to ask Emma to go with me. But I've been putting it off. Even though I know if I don't ask soon, it will be too late.

Me: So, the club is having a Christmas event tonight called 'Have A Red Christmas.' Everyone is to wear red. Want to go with me?

Emma: Sounds like fun. What time should I meet you there?

Me: I'll pick you up at seven.

No point in her driving there if I am going too. But this is a date and I'll be damned if I'm not picking her up.

The day seems to drag by as I wait for it to be time to pick her up. But it's all worth it when I pick her up and she steps out in a skintight red lace dress and a long, black coat. She looks stunning, but as she gets in the car, I can tell she's nervous.

As I start driving, I take her hand in mine, hoping to calm her down. The last thing I want is her nervousness.

"What's wrong, baby girl?"

"You not worried about people seeing us together?" She asks, and I'm not sure where she is going with this.

"No, I'm not. I'm proud to have you on my arm. If I'm being honest, I've been waiting a while for it."

She smiles but tries to hide it by looking out the window.

"What's on your mind?" I squeeze her hand.

"I'm just worried what people will think with you being Brody's brother."

He shrugs. "Fuck them. It's none of their business. If we are happy, so what?"

I know Brody will be an obstacle as we move forward.

"Is this just a holiday fling?"

"I don't want it to be," I admit.

It's heavy talk for a fun night, but if she needs to know, then I'll sit here all night and talk to her.

"Good, I'm glad we are on the same page," she says.

I squeeze her hand as we pull into the Club Red parking lot.

Walking into the club, there are red Christmas lights all over the place and everyone is in red. Most men are wearing a red button-down shirt and black pants like I am. Most of them have their shirts wide open, unlike I do. I figured on a date I shouldn't be on display for other women.

"See that couple over there at the bar?" I point out the older man with the younger woman. She looks, and then nods.

"That's Knox and his daughter's best friend, Summer. I'd say they had a bigger obstacle to overcome than we do. Don't you think? That couple over there on the couch? That's Evan and Aspen. He's her ex-boyfriend's father. Compared to them, I'd say you being my brother's ex is nothing."

"Around here it seems like it's nothing, but the first time I go to your parents for dinner... well, that won't be easy. Most likely it'll be awkward."

"You let me worry about that, okay? Tonight, we are here just to have fun. How about we go

JINGLE HIS BELLS

see the new themed room they made just for tonight?" I suggest.

"What is it?" She looks interested.

"It's bell themed, like jingle bells."

I lead her upstairs and point out some of the other themed rooms we didn't get to see last time, including the classroom and the doctor's office before we get to tonight's specially decorated room.

Bells are being used in every aspect of the room, from hanging on nipple clamps to hanging off vibrators, to being used in ball gags.

"I don't think I will look at a single bell the same again. Or be able to keep a straight face when 'Jingle Bells' comes on." She says, referring to the music playing overhead.

We watch a few scenes for a while and wander through a few of the rooms content to watch tonight. But by the time we head home, we can't keep our hands off each other.

"Come back to my place tonight," I ask.

When she agreed, I didn't think I could get us there fast enough. Even though I may not be able to tell Emma exactly how I feel, I sure as hell plan to show it tonight with every touch of her body.

Chapter 8

Emma

Brody and Zion's parents host a neighborhood Christmas party and it's tonight.

"You are going, right?" Kayla asks.

"I don't know. Zion didn't ask me to and with Brody and I split, I'm not sure if I should."

"You are going." My mom says in her don't argue with me voice and I guess that is that.

"How about this? We will get ready, and I'll go with you. We can make the rounds, say hi, then leave early and come back here to watch some Christmas movies." Kayla says looking at my mom.

"That's fine. So long as you say hi to everyone," Mom says.

They head out and Kayla and I finish getting ready in my room. I'm a nervous wreck and wonder if I should have texted Zion to let him know I was coming, so I reach for my phone.

"What are you doing?" Kayla snatches my phone from me.

"Thinking I should give Zion a heads up that I'm coming."

"Girl, you have been there every year since we were in sixth grade. If he doesn't know you are coming, then he's an idiot." She says, pocketing my phone.

Kayla drives us a few streets over to Zion and Brody's parents' house and we get a parking spot relatively close as someone else leaves.

Kayla and I walk in arm in arm and start greeting people. A few are shocked to see me here, while a few give me a thumbs up for coming to the party. All of these seem like really weird reactions until I get into the family room. There I find Brody with the girl from his study group sitting in his lap.

Kayla freezes beside me. With the way they are interacting, I can tell it's not a new relationship. Then I see Zion across the room looking guilty as hell. The entire room freezes. All I see is Zion's face, and all I hear is that stupid 'Jingle Bells' song playing on the radio.

"He knew. All long he knew," I whisper.

This whole time, Zion knew about Brody's new girl. This wasn't just 'oh we drifted apart,' this was he found someone else. Even if that was the case, he had deliberately strung me along.

The breakup didn't hurt. But the cheating does. And Zion knew.

I turn on my heel and walk right back out the front door with Kayla right behind me.

Zion is right on my heels as we reach the front yard. "Emma wait," Zion calls out.

"You knew, didn't you?" I spin around to face him.

"You were taking the break up so well I didn't want to ruin it."

"More like you didn't want to ruin the chance to get into my pants." I try to walk off again, but this time he grabs my hand.

When I turn around, I catch Brody coming out the front door heading right to us.

"That's not it at all and I know you don't believe that," Zion says.

"What I can't believe is you knew about Brody and have been fucking me all week and keeping me your dirty little secret. No matter how much you said you don't care who sees us together, well, no one saw us together!"

"What the fuck, Zion?" Brody roars across the lawn.

Zion closes his eyes for a brief moment and holds my hand tighter.

"How long have you been fucking my brother and cheating on me?" Brody turns to me.

"Are you fucking kidding me? You brought home for Christmas the girl you were cheating on me with and only broke up with me once we were all here in town via text message. I didn't fucking cheat on you, but go ahead and try to make yourself feel better," I yell at him while trying to pull my hand from Zion's, but he won't drop it.

"You only broke up with her because I pushed the issue," Zion interrupts. "You had no plans to. How you were going to hide the new girl I have no idea. What pisses me off even more is you said you'd do it in person, yet you did it via text. She deserved so much more than that," Zion says.

"It was none of your business," Brody yells.

"Yes, it was. I've had feelings for Emma before you even asked her out. But you made a move and liked her, so I locked them up. I wasn't about to sit there and watch you treat her like shit. When I met her that night at the club and heard how you broke up with her, I was pissed at you and relieved she was finally free. Not even you would hold me back this time." Zion finally drops my hand and Kayla is right there to take it.

Zion and Brody are full on fighting with each other in the middle of the front yard, so much so both his parents and mine walk out the door to see what is going on. My eyes lock with my mom's when they grow wide once she realizes what is going on.

"Come on, we are out of here," Kayla says as she pulls me toward her car.

"Thelma and Louise are out of here," Kayla yells loudly so that anyone who cares can hear.

Though I think most everyone is focused on Zion and Brody right now. People will be talking about this Christmas for years to come.

Chapter 9

Zion

I had this whole speech prepared for Emma when I gave her my Christmas gift. One that would tell her exactly how I felt about her. Only it all blew up in my face last night and instead of spending Christmas Eve with Emma and her family enjoying the holiday, I'm here feeling like shit because of everything that went down last night.

Even though I wanted her at my side at the party more then I wanted my next breath, but with Brody and Candy there it didn't seem right. Part of me was hoping she'd skip the party this year with everything going on, while the other part of me knew her parents wouldn't allow that.

Now I sit here staring at what I thought was the perfect Christmas gift.

One year, back when Emma was in the eighth grade, Brody and I were at her house for a weekend when my parents were out of town. We were playing around like brothers do and we broke one of her Christkindl Market mugs.

These mugs come out only at Christmas and they change every year. She was so sad and tried to hide it behind a wobbly tear-filled smile. It broke my heart. I think that was the moment I realized what I felt for her was bigger than a crush. But dating wasn't on either of our radars yet.

After that first night at the club when I talked to Hunter, I asked him for help. He has connections I don't and he was able to track down the mug Brody and I broke and he got it to me yesterday. I don't know how he did it, but I do know I owe him one.

Fuck it. I need to know I did everything I could and above all I want her to have this gift. I pick it up and make my way over to her house. If nothing else, it's a good excuse to check on her and maybe even get to talk to her for a moment.

When her dad opens the door, he doesn't say a word. Instead, he just stares at me and I don't blame him.

"I still want to give her the gift I got her. Right now, I know it's all fucked up, but I don't know where to start. I hope this is it." I hold up the wrapped gift.

He nods and steps back into the house. I come inside but don't move out of the entryway.

"Emma, come here a moment." He calls down the hall.

I can hear her and Kayla in the kitchen making Christmas cookies, judging by the scent of them filling the house. She is actually laughing, and I hope I'm doing the right thing.

Emma steps into the hallway in sweatpants and I swear she looks so damn beautiful it makes my heart ache.

"You don't have to talk to me, but I wanted to make sure you got your gift."

"It won't change anything," she says.

Just hearing her voice heals me even though it's not the words I want to hear. "I know and that's okay, but I got this for you and want you to have it." I hold out her gift and she takes a few hesitant steps before taking it from me.

"My feelings for you won't ever change, Emma. They have only grown stronger over time. Call me any time day or night. I'm yours."

Then I turn and walk out the door without looking back.

· · · · • · • • · ·

Emma

I stand there watching him go and my heart wants me to run after him and jump into his arms where I feel safe and wanted. But my head is too stubborn to allow that.

Going back to the kitchen, I set the gift on to the counter and Kayla gives me a look. Right then, I know I won't like what she has to say.

"You should at least open the present. If you are going to write him off, you should have all the facts," she says.

"I agree," Mom says, walking into the kitchen.

I look at the gift but shake my head and walk back to where we were making cookies.

"In a week he's done more than Brody has in years. You aren't curious about what could be in the box?" Kayla says.

Of course when she puts it like that, I am anxious to open it. Finally, I give in and open the gift and am shocked to find the one missing Christkindl Market mug from my collection. The one Zion and Brody broke so many years ago.

Staring at it, I'm shocked that he even remembered. I never brought it up when we were at the Christkindl Market this week so he had to have remembered from years ago. He's been paying attention longer then I thought.

"I have to go talk to him." I run upstairs, put on clean clothes and grab his gift before racing out the door.

Chapter 10

Zion

Back home, I ignore everything. My mom's texts and my dad's calls. My brother and his girl decided to go back to school today, so I know I won't hear from him.

I can't stop thinking of Emma and how badly I screwed up. She will go back to school, graduate and do amazing things and probably just think of this weekend as a learning experience. Maybe even write it off as a vacation fling. Years from now, she'll laugh about it with friends over a drink.

Meanwhile, I will still be trying to get over her, to convince myself it was only a onetime thing and not my only chance at the girl I've been in love with a lot longer than I even realized. I'm debating crawling into bed for the rest of the day when my doorbell rings.

JINGLE HIS BELLS 59

I assume it's my mom who got tired of me ignoring her and I almost don't answer it. But when the ringing starts again and much more incessantly, I open the door ready to yell at whoever is on the other side.

What I don't expect is to find Emma on the other side. Seeing her, my heart starts to race. She's here and I hope that's a good sign.

When I step back to invite her inside, she's hesitant. But I send up a silent prayer and she enters. I'm hoping that it's good news and she hasn't come to toss the mug at my head.

"I wanted to give you your gift too," She hands me a wrapped box.

She looks nervous as I slowly open the box and my eyes start to water.

One of the best Christmas presents I got growing up was a puppy. My little Boston terrier, Molly. She died last year, and it was really hard on me. I left her collar on my dresser at my parents' house because I wanted to keep it, but it was too hard to bring it here.

Inside the box is a picture of Molly on a wood plaque with two little paw prints and her collar attached. This picture is my all-time favorite of hers. She is sitting on my lap as we watch TV. Emma took this photo a few years ago and when she sent it to me, I framed it immediately and not just because she took it.

Emma steps up and wipes tears from my face I hadn't even realized were falling.

"I love you, Zion and I spent all last night thinking. While I'm still upset, I understand why you did it. If I put myself in your shoes, in the end, I'd have made the same choice."

This amazing and beautiful girl loves me. Fuck if that isn't the most amazing thing in the world.

"I love you too. I have for a lot longer than I should have."

When her lips land on mine, I feel like I'm finally whole, and it's an earth shattering feeling. My soul has found its home and I can't let her get away.

"You are mine now, baby girl, and I take care of what is mine, always."

"I hope so because I'm not going anywhere."

Epilogue

Emma

1 Year Later

Tonight is Club Red's Christmas party, and like last year, we are all in red. Once again, they have the bell room, but in addition, they also have a candy cane room. We have kept our membership to the club and make it a point to come and play at least once a month. More so now that I've graduated.

Since last Christmas, Zion hasn't left my side. He rented us a small apartment off-campus so we could live together, and he wouldn't have to be apart from me. Most of his work is done online so he can work anywhere and he said he was going to work near me.

He was my biggest cheerleader and was right there when I needed help to study or to have a relaxing night out. Kayla loved it because she hated her roommate and was over at our place all the time, and Zion didn't care. He made up a small bed in his office for her to stay any time she wanted.

After graduation, he sent me on not one, but two vacations. The first was a girl's weekend with Kayla to a beach in Florida and the other a weeklong trip to the mountains in Colorado with him.

In short, my life with Zion has been pretty perfect. We have had very few fights. For us, we prefer to talk things out before they blow up. As for family dinners at his parents, they have been a bit awkward with Brody since Candy didn't stick around long after last year's drama. Especially when she saw how much Brody's parents preferred me over her. Last I heard, she even transferred schools to be closer to home.

All in all, last year was the eye opener I needed on a few things, including that I was with the wrong brother. Zion showed me how I should be treated, and he kept raising the bar. Like tonight.

Zion and I didn't play last year, but we decided to have a little fun in the bell room tonight. He had my hands tied to the four-poster bed behind me. I'm standing at the edge of the bed in my red bra and panty set he insisted I wear. He has one of the vibrators in my pussy, driving me absolutely crazy.

Tonight we're putting on a little show for anyone who wants to watch it.

As a member of the club, I've become more and more confident and we have been getting more public each time. So when he makes me cum, I let myself go, giving myself over to it and don't think about everyone watching.

When I come back to consciousness, he's releasing my arms and wrapping me in a blanket. He carries me out of the room to one of the rooms dedicated for aftercare and we sit on an oversized chair while I snuggle into him.

"You were beautiful in there." He whispers in my ear.

"It was really fun."

"Each and every time we are here, I watch your trust in me grow. I can't explain how much that means to me. But I want to spend the rest of my life earning your complete trust. Will you marry me?"

For a moment, I'm in complete shock as it sinks in what he just asked me. When I sit up to look at him, he has a ring in his hand that I'm pretty sure could sink a small ship. It glitters in the low light and takes my breath away.

"Zion… " I whisper and for a moment when my eyes lock with his, words fail me.

"Yes!" I almost shout and wrap my arms around his neck before he takes my hand and places the ring on it. The ring that fits me like a glove.

"Come on, baby girl, let's go home and celebrate properly."

・・・・●・●・・・・

Want Kayla's story? Find her in Club Red starting with **Elusive Dom**!

Want more Emma and Zion? **Get an exclusive bonus epilogue**!

Other Books by Kaci Rose

See all of Kaci Rose's Books

Oakside Military Heroes Series
Saving Noah – Lexi and Noah
Saving Easton – Easton and Paisley
Saving Teddy – Teddy and Mia
Saving Levi – Levi and Mandy
Saving Gavin – Gavin and Lauren
Saving Logan – Logan and Faith

Oakside Shorts
Saving Mason - Mason and Paige
Saving Ethan – Bri and Ethan

Mountain Men of Whiskey River
Take Me To The River – Axel and Emelie
Take Me To The Cabin – Pheonix and Jenna
Take Me To The Lake – Cash and Hope
Taken by The Mountain Man - Cole and Jana
Take Me To The Mountain – Bennett and Willow
Take Me To The Edge – Storm

Chasing the Sun Duet
Sunrise – Kade and Lin
Sunset – Jasper and Brynn

Rock Stars of Nashville
She's Still The One – Dallas and Austin

Club Red – Short Stories
Daddy's Dare – Knox and Summer
Sold to my Ex's Dad - Evan and Jana
Jingling His Bells – Zion and Emma

Club Red: Chicago
Elusive Dom

Standalone Books
Texting Titan - Denver and Avery
Accidental Sugar Daddy – Owen and Ellie
Stay With Me Now – David and Ivy
Midnight Rose - Ruby and Orlando
Committed Cowboy – Whiskey Run Cowboys
Stalking His Obsession - Dakota and Grant
Falling in Love on Route 66 - Weston and Rory
Billionaire's Marigold - Mari and Dalton

Connect with Kaci Rose

Website

Facebook

Kaci Rose Reader's Facebook Group

TikTok

Instagram

Twitter

Goodreads

Book Bub

Join Kaci Rose's VIP List (Newsletter)

About Kaci Rose

Kaci Rose writes steamy contemporary romance mostly set in small towns. She grew up in Florida but longs for the mountains over the beach.

She is a mom to 5 kids and a dog who is scared of his own shadow.

She also writes steamy cowboy romance as Kaci M. Rose.

Please Leave a Review!

I love to hear from my readers! Please **head over to your favorite store and leave a review** of what you thought of this book!

Made in the USA
Columbia, SC
23 September 2024